→ A FABER PICTURE BOOK ←

Squishy McFluff

The Invisible Cat

Tea with the Queen

For
Jason
Corker,
dearly
missed.
Gxx

For SE,
HC, PA,
OJ and our
(visible)
cat.
E.O.

Pip Jones · Ella Okstad

90 YEARS OF EXCELLENCE

This is Squishy McFluff. He's a cat.

Squishy McFluff is Ava's cat.
Her INVISIBLE cat.

Squishy McFluff is
the best kitten EVER.
He's full of ideas and
ever so clever.

He's fluffy and tiny,
with pattering paws.
He knows lots of ways
to have fun on all fours!

We do bouncing!
And bowling!
And **yelling!**
And hopping!

And swinging! And skating!
And falling! And flopping!

And jumping! And scrumping!
And climbing! And hiding!
And running!
And rrrripping!

And slipping!

And sliding!

"Now hurry up, Squishy!"

He's off to get changed!
We're off on a trip that
my mum has arranged.

I want to be smart and he wants to be pretty,
'cos we're going to London, our capital city!

Look all around!
The big churches! And towers!
A market where people sell
nothing but flowers!

A square with a fountain
and statues of cats!
And . . .

a palace with guards wearing tall, furry hats!

Let's go IN! Oh, we can't . . .

because of my sister.
She needs a quick snack.
And my dad's got a blister!

Oh, this will take AGES. And waiting's a BORE!
Squishy and I really want to explore.

"Squish, that's a super,
FANTASTIC idea!
We should go in
while the others stay here."

Hooray! How exciting! Just look at that guard,
strutting around in the palace front yard.

And what's this arriving?
A big, fancy car!

"Wait . . . what's that, Squishy? There's a door that's ajar?"
He wants to go in 'cos he says he has heard
tales of a royal **dog** whose life is absurd!

The dog is called Corgi . . .
she has her own cook!
Let's try and find her,
we'll sneak in and look.

That must be Corgi!
She looks very cosy
there on her velvety cushion, all dozy.

Squish wants to wake her.
He has a great plan . . .
But who is this lady?
She looks like my nan!

She's reading aloud
from a handwritten sheet,
and asking the dog what she fancies to eat.
Beef wellington? Ham hock?
Roast chicken? A steak?
Mineral water or
a doggie-choc shake?

"Squish, why are you pointing?"
Ooh, her hat! It's quite bold,
with the sparkly bits, and the fabric and gold . . .
Oh, crumpets! A CROWN! That must be the QUEEN!
We'd better go quickly, before we are seen!

Uh-oh. Too late!

"Er, I say! Who are YOU?

And how DID you get in?

Did the guards let you through?"

"Hello, Mrs Queen! It's only me, Ava.
I'm ever so sorry, could you do me a favour?
Your shoes are the best ones that I ever saw,
but please take your foot off my cat's little paw."

"What cat, young lady?
I can't see him! Where?"
"Behind you, my Majesty –
sitting right THERE!"

"You're really just not looking quite HARD enough. He's THERE, Mrs Queen! SEE?! It's Squishy McFluff!"

"Well, good gracious, Ava!"

"All through my reign,
I've dined out with kings,
drunk the finest champagne.
I've seen many wonders,
all the world over
(the world's biggest sapphire,
a HUGE four-leaf clover).

I thought I'd seen EVERYTHING . . . well! Fancy that!
Even I've never seen an INVISIBLE cat!"

"How lucky you are! Ava, do stay for tea.
I'd be HONOURED if you'd both dine here with me.
I could ask my best chefs if they'd whip up a roast?
Or perhaps my own favourite? Hot cheese on toast!"

"What a scrumm-YUMtious feast!"
I'm so full. So is Squish!
He's eaten **nineteen**
huge invisible fish!

It's time to go home now,
it's getting quite late.
"Thanks, Mrs Queen! Oh,
the meal was just great."

"What fun to meet such an imaginative girl!
You're now a Duchess, and McFluff is an Earl,
and both of you MUST take home one of these, dear!
It's just a small present, a royal souvenir."

Wow, look how it sparkles!
My very own crown.
And one for Squish too . . .
though it's on upside-down!

Back home again – phew! Ava's already snoring!
Well, a day out with Squishy could . . .

never be
boring!